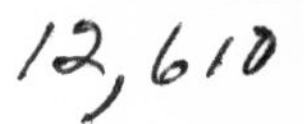

Anderson, C. W.

Blaze and the gray spotted pony, story and pictures by C. W. Anderson. Macmillan, c1968.

47 p. illus. (A Billy and Blaze book)

Tommy is ready when he gets his own pony because Billy and his horse Blaze have helped him to learn to ride and care for horses.

1. Horses - Stories   I. Title

A Billy and Blaze Book

BLAZE AND THE GRAY SPOTTED PONY

BLAZE and the GRAY SPOTTED PONY

Story and Pictures

by C. W. ANDERSON

COLLIER BOOKS
DIVISION OF MACMILLAN PUBLISHING CO., INC.
NEW YORK

COLLIER MACMILLAN PUBLISHERS
LONDON

Macmillan Publishing Co., Inc., 866 Third Avenue, New York, N.Y. 10022
Collier Macmillan Canada Ltd.

ISBN 0-02-041480-3

Library of Congress catalog card number: 68-10997
Blaze and the Gray Spotted Pony *is published in a hardcover edition by Macmillan Publishing Co., Inc.*
Printed in the United States of America

First Collier Books Edition 1974

10 9 8 7 6 5 4 3

to Billy, David and Christopher

Tommy was a little boy who loved horses.
Almost all his dreams were about
horses—all kinds of horses.

Tommy's father and mother and uncles and aunts had never had to ask what he wanted for his birthday or for Christmas. They knew.

Once Tommy got a beautiful horse for his birthday. It was almost as big as a pony, and he could ride it. Its mane and coat felt real. It wasn't alive, of course—but almost.

Billy, who lived down the road, had a beautiful pony named Blaze. Tommy always watched when they rode by. Billy always waved to him and he waved back.

Whenever Tommy got a new little toy horse he always showed it to Billy. Billy said they were very nice and looked real.

Sometimes Billy let Tommy ride on Blaze as he led him over the fields. He taught Tommy how to sit in the saddle and hold tight with his legs.

Billy also showed Tommy how to take care of a pony. He knew that Tommy wanted to learn this because maybe some day he would have a pony of his own.

Often Tommy ran along beside Blaze when Billy went for a ride, but after a while he got tired and turned back. How he wished he had a real pony of his own!

One day when Tommy was out with Billy they saw a little spotted pony in a field. When the pony saw them he whinnied and Tommy whinnied back. He loved that little gray spotted pony at once.

After that Tommy's dreams were only of a gray spotted pony that always whinnied to him. Tommy always whinnied back.

One day Tommy's father and mother noticed that he was very busy building something in the backyard.

When it was almost finished they came to look
at it. "It looks something like a house,"
said Tommy's father.
"It's a stable for my pony," said Tommy,
"if I get one for my birthday. Gray, with
spots—and alive."

The next day Tommy's father went and asked Billy to help him. "I want to get a pony for Tommy's birthday," he said. "Gentle, like Blaze, but small and gray with spots." He knew it would not be easy.

Tommy's father drove his car and Billy followed behind on Blaze. They went to many farms but most of the ponies were too big for a little boy.

And many were too wild and lively for a boy just beginning to ride.

And none were gray with spots. Both Billy and Tommy's father were sad when they started for home. Tomorrow was Tommy's birthday and they had no pony for him.

Just then Blaze gave a loud snort and started
to pull away. Tommy's father and Billy
turned and saw a trailer going by.
A little pony was putting his head out of
the back. He was gray—and he had spots.

112

The man driving the trailer saw Billy wave to him and stopped. While Blaze and the gray pony made friends Tommy's father talked to the man and found he was going to sell the pony.

"This pony is too small for my boy now and I must get him a bigger one," the man said.

So Tommy's father bought the pony. Afterward he asked Billy to take the pony home with him so Tommy wouldn't see him until his birthday.

The next morning when Tommy came outdoors
he saw Billy riding toward him on Blaze—
and he was leading a pony! The pony was
gray and he had spots! He whinnied when
he saw Tommy and Tommy whinnied back.

"Blaze found a gray spotted pony for you," said Billy.

Tommy soon had his arms around the pony's neck. "You're mine," he said, "and you're just like the pony in my dream."

When Tommy rode his pony beside Blaze
through the woods he knew he was the
happiest boy in the world. This was his
very own pony—gray, with spots, and alive.